LET'S PLAY GONGGI

Let's Play Gonggi

Brown Books Kids
Dallas / New York
www.BrownBooksKids.com
(972) 381-0009

A New Era in Publishing®

Publisher's Cataloging-In-Publication Data
Names: Im, Seo-Ha., author. | Kim, Minjoo, illustrator.
Title: Let's play gonggi / Im Seo-Ha ; illustrated by Minjoo Kim.
Description: Dallas ; New York : Brown Books Kids, [2023] | Interest age level: 006-010. |
    Summary: A whole class. Five pebbles. Two professionals, and a girl who refuses to learn the
    game. Who will win the gonggi tournament?--Publisher.
Identifiers: ISBN: 9781612545820 (hardcover) | LCCN: 2022945990
Subjects: LCSH: Games--Competitions--Juvenile fiction. | Pebbles--Juvenile fiction. | Play—
Juvenile fiction. | Friendship--Juvenile fiction. | Learning--Juvenile fiction. | CYAC: Games--
    Competitions--Fiction. | Pebbles--Fiction. | Play--Fiction. | Friendship--Fiction. | Learning--
    Fiction. | BISAC: JUVENILE FICTION / Sports & Recreation / Games. | JUVENILE FICTION /
    Social Themes / Friendship.
Classification: LCC: PZ7.1.I377 Le 2023 | DDC: [E]--dc23

This book has been officially leveled by using the
F&P Text Level Gradient™ Leveling System.

ISBN 978-1-61254-582-0
LCCN 2022945990

Printed in China
10 9 8 7 6 5 4 3 2 1

For more information or to contact the author, please go to
www.BrownBooksKids.com.

LET'S PLAY GONGGI

Im Seo-Ha

Illustrated by Minjoo Kim

BROWN BOOKS KIDS

"Good morning, partner!"

Eunji's smile faded as she entered the classroom.

"What a pretty dress, partner!" Jingu exclaimed. "You look like a princess."

She wished he would stop calling her "partner," but he wouldn't. She wondered why their teacher paired her with him.

"Partner! There seems to be something in your pocket. What are those? Aren't they gonggidols?"

"In my pocket?" Eunji felt inside her pocket and pulled out a small collection of stones.

"Wow, they really are gonggidols! So cool! I wonder how well the kids in Seoul play gonggi." Jingu came from the countryside in Gyeongsang-do, and he was popular among the children because of his accent.

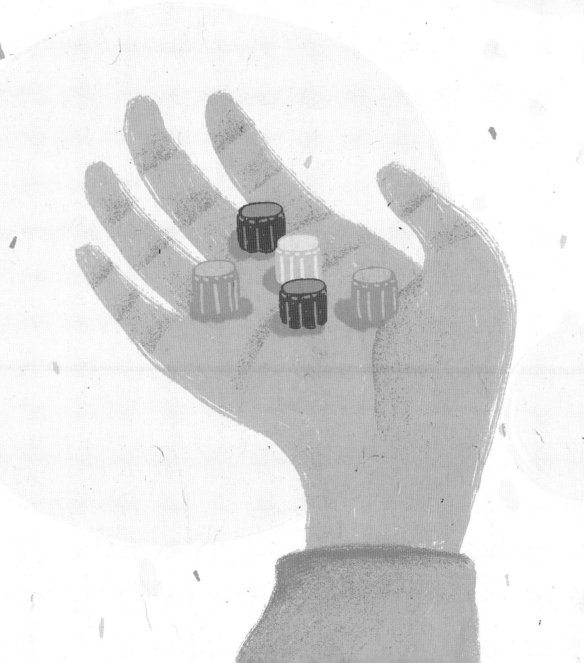

"Eunji! Why don't you start playing?

"I—I am . . ." Eunji's face got redder by the second. When she had borrowed her sister's dress that morning without permission, she had never imagined there would be gonggidols in the pocket!

"Don't tell me that you don't know how to play gonggi. Come on, Eunji! Try it."

"I bet she doesn't know anything about playing gonggi," said Jingu.

Not waiting for Eunji, Jingu began to play. He rolled the gonggidols on the desk, and the colorful stones flew up and down like trapeze artists performing aerial tricks.

"Wow, fantastic!" the children exclaimed.

All the children were amazed, but Jingu snorted and said, "In my hometown, this is nothing. Every little kid can do this, no sweat."

"I used to play gonggi with pebbles. Compared to them, these gonggidols are very colorful. Look! At first, you catch one stone at a time, and then two at a time, and then three . . ."

After his demonstration, every kid tried to catch gonggidols, but Eunji—who was pouting—refused to touch them.

I will never play gonggi in my life! she thought stubbornly.

"You're right, Jingu! This is really fun!"
said one of the other children.
"It's much more fun than playing with
toys or cards, isn't it?" Jingu responded.

In the middle of playing, Sungil had an idea.
"I heard that the class next to us will
have a ddakji competition. How about we
have a gonggi competition?" he suggested.
"Gonggi competition?" asked Jingu.

From that day on, all the kids were practicing gonggi everywhere, all the time.

Click-click here and *clink-clink* there. The classroom was filled with the sound of children playing gonggi.

Eunji didn't like what she saw. Every day she was surrounded by gonggi. *What happened to all my friends?* she thought sullenly.

She trudged home. Her heavy footsteps were just like her heavy heart.

Everyone is playing only gonggi! This is all because of Jingu!

In anger, Eunji kicked a stone on the road.

"Ouch!" said an unknown voice.

Surprised, Eunji hid behind a lamppost.

"Partner, I bet you want to eat dalgona so badly!"

"Is that you, Jingu?"

He was sitting next to an old woman who was selling the honeycomb candy. "This dalgona tastes really good. Try it, partner."

"I won't. I never eat street foods."

But all of a sudden, she tasted sweetness as Jingu shoved a bit of dalgona in her mouth.

"What are you doing, Jingu?!"

"What do you think? Doesn't it taste like honey?"

"Not at all!" Eunji lied. As the sweetness disappeared, she felt she needed more.

"I was going to give you this fish-shaped yeot if you would play just one game of gonggi. But if you don't want to, I understand." Jingu showed her a big, fish-shaped taffy treat he had just received from the grandma.

"Wait a second!" It was the biggest yeot Eunji had ever seen. So she asked him, "Do you really mean it? If I play gonggi just once, you'll give it to me?"

"Yes! Here, these are the most wonderful pebbles I picked up from the creek in my hometown. Just give it a try!"

Eunji threw one stone up in the air and caught it with her hand.

"Wow! I caught it! I did it!" she exclaimed.

"Right, you did it! Great job! Why have you kept it a secret that you're so good at gonggi?" He paused. "I think I want to eat the yeot myself, but I promised to give it to you. So here you go." Jingu handed over the treat.

Though Eunji got the yeot, she still wanted something more—to play gonggi! So she said, "Jingu, why don't we play gonggi some more?"

"That's it! I knew you would want to play. Now it's my turn!"

They played and played and played some more. Even when the sun began to set, they never got tired of playing gonggi.

At last, the day of the gonggi competition came.

In the classroom, lots of children gathered for the competition. Some came to watch, others to play, but all were there for gonggi.

"Why hasn't Jingu come?" one of the children asked.

They waited for Jingu for so long, but he didn't show up.

Finally, Sungil said, "We can't wait anymore. We have to get started without him."

They decided to take turns drawing numbers out of a hat to determine which order they would compete in.

Eunji's heart pounded as she drew her number...
It was ten!

   *Ten means that I'll play last. It also means
that I must play against one of the best players.*
Thinking that she would surely lose, Eunji felt
discouraged and hopeless.

"If Jingu doesn't play, I might become the champion," said Sungil with confidence.
    Without Jingu, the competition was a total mess. Gonggidols were everywhere, and every kid insisted that he or she had won.

They managed to continue the competition until the last game: Eunji versus Sungil.

"I can easily defeat her. It'll be a piece of cake!" Sungil was about to toss a gonggidol when a voice filled the room.

"Just a minute!"

It was Jingu, with one arm wrapped in a cast.

"The last game should be played with true gonggidols, right?" Jingu asked. Jingu held out real stone gonggidols, not ones made of plastic.

"What? How can we play with pebbles?" asked Sungil.

"In my hometown, even little kids play with them," Jingu said.

Eunji quickly gathered the pebbles and tossed one up.

Sungil gasped. "Eunji! You couldn't play gonggi before, could you?"

When Eunji played gonggi, it looked like the gonggidols were dancing on the back of her hand.

"Wow! You're great!" the children exclaimed.

Jingu agreed. "You have practiced every day. Now you are good at gonggi, partner!"

Sungil seemed to be surprised by Jingu's words, but finally, he threw one pebble high.

The game between Eunji and Sungil lasted a long time.

"Oh no!" cried Eunji when one of her stones rolled away. The two stones were so far apart that it seemed like she couldn't grab them both at the same time. "What should I do? Should I give up?"

"Just try your best, partner! You don't know what will happen."

"Okay, I'll try!"

Eunji tossed one stone up high and ...

"Wow!"

"You did it!"

All the children cheered. Eunji was bursting with happiness. Jingu congratulated her with a big thumbs-up. Even Sungil, her opponent, smiled and clapped for her.

"Here comes the gonggi champion! Clear the way!" Jingu shouted in a silly voice. Every kid burst into laughter.

What if I hadn't worn my sister's dress? Eunji thought happily. She held the gonggidols tightly in her hand and whispered, "Thank you, gonggidols!"

Do You Want to Know About Gongginori? There weren't always colorful gonggidols made of plastic. Remember the pebbles Jingu brought from his hometown? In the old days, children just picked up any thumbnail-sized stones that were on the ground. Back then, anything from nature could be a toy for children. Now let's learn more about gongginori.

The Origin of Gongginori

Although its origin has not been clearly identified, *Ojuyeonmunjangjeonsango*, a book written during the reign of King Heonjong (1834–1849) of Korea, explains, "There is a game where children play with round stones called gonggi." This record shows that the origin of gongginori goes back hundreds of years!

How to Play Gongginori

Gongginori is played with small stones by two or more players. It can be played anywhere, indoors or outdoors.

While one person can play gonggi alone, usually multiple players compete with each other as individuals or in teams. Once teams are formed, players first draw numbers out of a hat or perform a round of rock-paper-scissors, or another game, to determine the order. Then, players decide on a number of points, and the first player to reach that number wins. Players earn one point for each completed level. If the stones on the ground are touched, or any of the stones on the back of the player's hand (see Level 5) fall, their turn is over, and the game moves on to the next player.

Level 1 — Clasping one stone

After throwing five stones on the ground, pick up a stone and throw it up in the air.

While it is airborne, pick up one stone from the ground and catch the falling stone. Repeat these steps until all five stones are in hand.

Level 2 — Clasping two stones

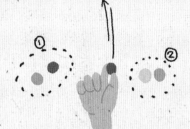

Pick up two stones from the ground after throwing one stone up in the air and catch the falling stone. Repeat until all five stones have been gathered.

Level 3 — Clasping three stones

Throw one stone in the air and pick up three stones. After catching the falling stone, throw a stone in the air again, pick up another from the ground, and catch the falling stone.

Level 4 — Clasping four stones

With all five stones in hand, throw one stone up in the air and put the remaining four stones on the ground before catching the stone in midair. Throw the stone in the air again, pick up the four stones on the ground, and catch the falling stone.

SO EASY!

Level 5 — Kkeokgi

After completing Levels 1 through 4, toss the five stones from the palm of the hand into the air and swiftly turn the hand to catch the stones on the back of the hand.

Throw all the stones back in the air and snatch them with the palm side of the hand.

DIFFICULT!

ABOUT THE AUTHOR

Im Seo-Ha studied literature at university. After graduation, she worked as an editor for a publishing house. Still, the chattering little writer in her heart kept sticking her head out and writing.

As an active co-creator of Three People—a creative group specializing in children's books—she has written many books, including *Let's Play Ddakji*, *Let's Play Jegi*, and *Pick and Read Traditional Fairy Tales from Textbooks*.

ABOUT THE ILLUSTRATOR

Minjoo Kim majored in oriental painting in college and studied at the Kkokdu Illustration Academy. She's happiest when her imagination blooms into a story and she makes a picture book that can be enjoyed for a long time. Minjoo Kim is the author and illustrator of *On a Fever Night*, and she's illustrated several other books including the five volume environmental picture-book set and accompanying workbook, *Today's Fine Dust*, and *A Night with Fever*.